Drew's Fab Jab

TODAY
I WAS
BRAVE

Gregoire Hodder

Jamie Sugg

Cambridge Children's Books,
5 Winfold Road, Waterbeach,
Cambridge, CB25 9PR.

www.cambridgechildrensbooks.com

Drew's Fab Jab

Written by Gregoire Hodder and Illustrated by Jamie Sugg

This is Drew, a very little mouse,

But Drew's heart is as big as a house.

You will often see a smile on Drew's face.

Drew's jacket is green and has gold buttons; it's ace.

This is Drew's Dad, who has some news.
"It's not that bad, so don't get the blues.
Drew, today you need to have a jab.
It's important, and it won't be that bad."

Off Drew went to the docs for a jab.

Drew knew Dad was right but needed to think.

Drew didn't really want to cause a stink,

But the mouse was a little scared.

The mouse was a little unprepared.

Drew went to see Owl, who was teaching at school.

Owl is wise and clever, which is pretty cool.

"Dad said I need to get a jab," said Drew.

Owl said, "Let me show you why that is true!"

"Twitt-twoo little mouse, you should get a jab, yes.
Jabs can cause you a little stress,
But they're great and can help stop you getting sick.
So, it's worth it; it will do the trick."

Off Drew went to the docs to have a jab.
Drew knew Owl was right but needed to think.
Drew didn't really want to cause a stink,
But the mouse was still a little scared.
The mouse was still a little unprepared.

On the way there, through the wildwood.
The mouse saw Badger and knew he was good.
"Badger, I'm a bit scared," said the mouse sadly,
"I have to get a jab. Will it hurt badly?"

"Oh, little mouse, jabs used to fill me with dread.
When I was younger, I was scared too," Badger said.
"What? Not Badger, surely not you!
You are so big and strong," said Drew.

"I'm not scared anymore," said Badger politely.
"Let me tell you it did hurt, BUT only slightly.
More of a scratch, more like a pinch,
Afterwards, I realised it was a cinch!"

Off Drew went to the docs to have a jab.

Drew knew Badger was right but needed to think.

Drew didn't want to cause a stink,

But the mouse was still a little scared.

The mouse was still a little unprepared.

Health
Centre

The mouse left Badger feeling quite brave.

On mouse went and saw Dog, who gave him a wave.

Dog was smiling and always seemed happy,

His tail thumping on the ground - thwacky thwacky.

Drew said, "You always have a smile on your face,
I need to have a jab, and that's not ace."
"Well, when I had mine, guess what I did instead?
I thought of a joke and laughed and smiled," Dog said.

Dog settled back into his chair and told his joke.

"A mouse walks into a doctor's office. He has a cucumber up his nose, a carrot in his left ear, and a banana in his right ear. 'What's the matter with me?' the mouse asks the doctor. The doctor replies, 'You're not eating properly.'"

The mouse laughed harder than ever before.
Drew laughed so much and had never laughed more.
Dog said, "when you get jabbed, remember that smile,
It will make it easier by a mile."

Off Drew went to the docs to have a jab.

Drew knew that Dog was right but needed to think.

Drew didn't want to cause a stink,

But the mouse was still a little scared.

The mouse was still a little unprepared.

Mouse saw Cat, who was always at her best.
Whatever Cat did, Cat never seemed stressed.
"I need a jab and want to talk to you,
I am feeling a bit unprepared," said Drew.

Cat said, "Hello mouse when I have a jab,
I stretch, then breathe deep and feel fab.
I will show you, just do like I do.
Stretch out your back until it feels like new."

Cat said, "I breathe in, then breathe out nice and slow,
Then stretch and roll my shoulders high, then low,
and let my arms hang loose and floppy - it's fab!
I am so relaxed I hardly notice when they jab."

That sounded great to the mouse, who felt good.

Drew then arrived at the doctors in the wood.

Drew did not feel like a scared little mouse.

Drew felt brave, confident and big as a house.

Health Centre

Drew knew Cat was right and gave it some thought.

There was no reason to be distraught.

The mouse was no longer scared.

The mouse was totally prepared.

Mummy Mouse was waiting at the docs for Drew.

Drew said, "I'm ready; I can do this; it's true!"

"I'm proud of you; give me a hug," Mummy Mouse said.

So off into the doctors, they sped.

The doctor and nurse were very nice,
They were used to looking after little mice.
They let Drew sit in a giant blue chair,
And treated the mouse with lots of care.

Drew thought of Owl and remembered to be wise.
Drew thought of big Badger and felt twice the size.
Drew thought of Dog's joke and began to laugh.
Drew was already feeling better by half.

Drew thought of Cat, stretched, breathed deep and slow.
Drew's shoulders rolled, and arms hung loose and low.
The Nurse rolled up Drew's sleeve and took Drew's arm.
Drew felt a slight scratch but stayed very calm.

KEEP
FIT

Now Badger was right - it did hurt a bit,

But not too much, he had to admit.

After they covered Drew's arm,

They gave Drew a sticker that worked like a charm.

Drew's new sticker was for being so good.

Dad came, and they all walked home through the wood.

The mouse was now happy; Drew had got the jab.

Drew was so pleased and felt totally fab!

Comprehension

Getting a jab can be a little stressful, but they're great and can help stop you from getting very sick.

If you get a bug, it can make you unwell. Getting a jab will give you a vaccine that can help your body fight the bug.

How do you think Drew felt when Daddy Mouse said Drew had to get a jab?

How do you think Drew felt after getting the jab?

What do you think helped Drew the most with getting the jab?

TODAY I WAS BRAVE

Printed in Great Britain
by Amazon